# A Round of Robins

## *A Joy Forest Cozy Mystery*

# *The Novella*

### *Blythe Ayne*

# A Round of Robins
## The Novella

**Blythe Ayne**

**Emerson & Tilman, Publishers**
**129 Pendleton Way #55**
**Washougal, WA 98671**

www.BlytheAyne.com
Blythe@BlytheAyne.com

### A Round of Robins - The Novella
ebook ISBN:         978-1-957272-61-0
Paperback ISBN:     978-1-957272-62-7
Large Print ISBN:   978-1-957272-63-4
Audio ISBN:         978-1-957272-64-1

[**FICTION** / Mystery & Detective / Cozy / General
**FICTION** / Mystery & Detective / Women Sleuths
**FICTION** / Mystery & Detective / Cozy / Cats & Dogs]

**BIC: FM**

# A Round of Robins

## *A Joy Forest Cozy Mystery*

## *The Novella*

*Blythe Ayne*

# DEDICATION:

*To All Who Enjoy Exploring*
*Mysteries of Mind & Heart*

*The year is 2032....*

Although the times are different, mystery and romance are ever the same. This is Joy's world – *come on in!*

# *A Round of Robins*

I was deep in my research of the *Coastal First Nations People*, listening to Chief Dan George recite a heart-warming prayer to nature, when my computer softly dared to interrupt, "Detective Travis Rusch...."

"Tell him I'm not available," I ordered.

"Dr. Forest is not available," Computer told Travis.

Much to my irritation, he employed his police online override. "Joy? I know you're there."

"Pause," I told the neural net. The 3-D image of the Salish chief standing in the forest froze in place, surrounding me. "Just because my body is sitting here in the midst of my neural net, Travis, does not mean that I'm actually here."

"Oh," Travis said, amused. "Where are you?"

"In the forest," I answered, "documenting a heart-stirring prayer to nature by a Salish chief."

There was a long pause from Travis. I tapped my foot. "*Well?*"

"In the forest … so sorry to bother you, I guess you're working.…"

"Usually. You know that."

"I do. Yes."

"It'd be great if you thought a bit more about me," I blurted.

"*Hmmm.* It isn't so much I need to think about you *more* as to think about you *differently.*"

Goodness! That comment brought a wrinkle to my brow, but I set it aside. "As charming as this conversation is," I said, with a slight twinge of sarcasm, "I assume you didn't call for idle chat."

Robbie, my robot cat, sensing my frustration, stalked around my chair, swishing his tail. "It's okay Robbie."

"What's up with Robbie?"

"He's picking up on my irritation at being interrupted. He's tail swishing around my chair. Which is a bit like I'm feeling."

"Tail swishing?" Travis asked, with a chuckle.

"That did not come out quite like I meant." I stood and started to pace back and forth in my little bedroom. I wondered how he had the time to lollygag like this, but I refused to bring up a visual. Seeing him would distract me even more. "Where are you?"

"I'm in the dog park. I have the afternoon off. So… I decided to get away from it all, come to the dog park, you know, and watch the dogs, hoping to set aside, for a few minutes at least, the case I'm working on that's driving me nuts. And I brought with me that thing you got me."

"That thing I got you? What are you talking about?"

"That thing that runs on mind power."

"Oh! You mean the Mind-Boggler."

"Yeah. The Mind-Boggler."

"I gave that to you *ages* ago. I got it at the Invention Convention in Scotland."

"Right. I'm a bit embarrassed to confess that I only glanced at it when you gave it to me. I thought, 'I'll figure out what it is some other time,' then set it down and *completely* forgot about it.

"But today … it's such a bright and beautiful sunny day, and I have the afternoon off, which, as you know, is rare enough, that I decided to lay claim to *nothing* in a big way, come to the dog park, sit under a tree, and think about nothing."

"Bright sunny day?" It had rained nonstop, around the clock, for seven days. "*Shades, open!*" I commanded.

"*Yowl!*" Robbie flung his tail over his eyes, and I averted my eyes from the brilliant light.

"Sorry, Robbie!"

"Give a robot cat a warning, will ya!" He looked up at me over his tail.

"Again my little wonder-feline, I apologize. Are you adjusted?"

"I'*m blind!* Can't see a thing. Oh no, wait. Everything comes together. All right crisis averted. Visual orbs in working order." He stopped chattering and jumped up on the windowsill. "Hey! It's a beautiful sunny day! Let's go out and play!"

I chortled. "Poetry aside, dear Robbie, I have work to do. But you can go into the backyard if you want. See if Dickens wants to go with you."

Dickens, the bio-cat, slept in the middle of the bed as usual. He lazily opened one eye at the mention of his name, then closed it again.

"Or … not," I added.

"I'm sure I want to play all alone in the backyard," Robbie complained, "in the wet grass that has been rained on night and day for days on end. And, as you can see, Dickens is in his cat-land, not to be disrupted." Robbie gave me a disapproving look over his shoulder. "All by myself," he appended, milking it.

"*Hello,*" Travis said.

"Oh! Right." I'd gotten completely distracted by the sunlight. "Yes, Travis, you have the day off, it's a sunny day, you're at the dog park. Somehow that relates to the Mind-Boggler. Great mystery."

I joined Robbie at the window looking out into my side yard where the few primroses I'd planted were thriving. That was nice to know. I'd planted them and forgot about them. *Hmmm*, that might be the best way for me to handle plants as a rule.

"That's right, the Mind-Boggler," Travis carried on. "Although I'd decided to come to the dog park and do absolutely nothing, I know myself. If I came here with nothing to do, I wouldn't stay long. Then my eyes fell on the Mind-Boggler, patiently sitting on the corner of my desk all these weeks. So I brought it along."

"That's … nice." I remained bemused. *Why* was this bit of information so urgent that it had to take my precious workday? "*And so?…*"

"And so I found this lovely park bench under a spreading chestnut tree. There are hoards of dogs here. They're so fun to watch, all chasing after … whatever they're chasing after, their owners chatting in a friendly manner. It's a perfect, bucolic day. Anyway, after a bit, I got out the Mind-Boggler. And, Joy! It's the most amazing thing! Truly, it's the most amazing thing! Do you realize that?"

"Well, yes, I do. That's why I got it for you, I thought you might find it entertaining."

"It's more than entertaining. The instructions said to just think to it and it would do what I thought. I didn't quite believe it, but why not try? So I thought, 'come out of your little box.' And immediately it zipped up out of its box, hovering in front of me. Then I thought, 'become all the colors of the rainbow.' And it started shifting through all the colors of the rainbow. In fact, I think it was making some colors I can't even see."

"Yes, that's one of the things it does. It gradually floats into the range of colors we can't see. If you're open to it, it's possible to train yourself to see into those extreme color ranges."

"Astonishing!" Travis exclaimed. "Yes. Quite a sensation. I did feel as though I was looking at colors I can't quite see. Do you have a Mind-Boggler?"

"Yep. I interact with it a couple evenings during the week. It seems to work better for me when I'm really tired."

"*Cool!*" Travis said.

I was just the tiniest bit stunned. I'm not sure that I've ever heard Travis in such a fit of boy-like enthusiasm. "I'm glad you're enjoying it. It runs on your energy, you know."

"Yeah, it's spectacular. The thing is, not only was I enjoying the Mind-Boggler for personal entertainment, but I realized if it can expand my senses, it could help me in my detective work."

That's exactly what I'd thought when I decided to get a Mind-Boggler for him along with the one I got for myself at the Invention Convention. But I didn't, at that point, yet know if it worked as advertised. So I'd handed it to him unceremoniously and unwrapped, with the offhanded comment, "you might find this fun."

But *still!* Why did he have to tell me about his experience at *this precise moment*, while the mystical aura of the chief's chant faded? My inspired writing that was just beginning to come over me when Travis interrupted was disappearing, as well. Inspiration was frustrating that way.

"I have to tell you, Joy, when you handed me the Mind-Boggler, I was mystified by why you'd give me such a thing. It looked like a toy, and you didn't say what it could do ... so...."

"True. That's because I didn't know for sure what it could do. I saw it demonstrated at the Invention Convention, and it looked amazing. But, you know, maybe it *was* amazing, and maybe it was just a souped-up demonstration. Since you've never mentioned it, I never brought it up, either."

"Well, I'm mentioning it now! But ... there's ... another reason why I'm calling...."

*Aha!* Finally, we get to the *real* point! "Yes?"

"I feel like a first-class idiot...."

*Wow!* It was a rare day when Travis Rusch referred to himself in *any* deprecating terms. I wanted to tease him, but I couldn't bring myself to do it. Instead, I said, "I'm sure that's an exaggeration," really wishing I had turned on visual. What was the expression on his face when he referred to himself as an idiot?

*However!* The prayer to nature hung in mid-air, and I must return to my work. My deadline loomed, and my project was barely begun. Add to that the fact that there was nothing that derailed me more than Travis's distracting, incredible, kaleido-scopic hazel-green eyes. *Hammer and blast!* How could I get him to make his point so I could return to my work?

"I was having a delightful time," Travis continued. "And I'd moved from exploring colors to exploring sounds. I asked the Mind-Boggler to quietly imitate the sounds of the different dogs. Which it performed to perfection. Then, I noticed hundreds and *hundreds* of robins, industriously making their nests, chirping and singing! I had the thought that maybe the dogs kept cats away, which was why all the robins were here."

This made me laugh. "Brilliant, Travis!" Again, wishing to see his face, and almost succumbing to turning on visual. But I restrained myself.

"So," Travis continued, "I had the Mind-Boggler imitate the robins, all their chirps and tweets and calls. It was delightful! I never knew they made so many sounds. Of course, the next thought was to see if the Mind-Boggler could expand my sense of sound in the same way it seemed to have done with color. I was very engrossed in that discovery, but weirdly... and truly, Joy I don't understand it ... I dove into a deep, deep sleep! I mean, I hardly ever sleep deeply.

"Isn't that weird? Has this ever happened to you with the Mind-Boggler?"

"I can't say that it has, but I'm usually working with it when I'm headed for sleep anyway. There's no reason to be alarmed. It's your day off, it's warm and sunny, you're on a park bench surrounded by beautiful doggies and their charming owners. So, what's your concern?"

"True, that, yes. But … you see … the very strange thing is … when I woke up … the Mind-Boggler had *disappeared.* I've turned the place upside down looking for it. I've embarrassed myself by asking every single dog owner if I could look in the mouth of their pet. *Arg!* They've all left now because of the weird guy on the park bench."

*Holy moly, gluten-free macaroni!* This was not the Travis I've ever known or encountered! I was speechless. But then these words popped out of my mouth, "I hope you're not in uniform."

Travis uttered a dry little drawl of a laugh. "No, I'm not in uniform." He paused. "Will you *please* turn on visual?"

"I … *ahhh*, I'm not presentable," I lied. I glanced in the mirror. Well, maybe *not* a lie. "I'm sure it's there somewhere. But since the Mind-Boggler has the ability to transform itself, it's hard to tell what may have happened to it."

"*Oh, oh, oh,* I hadn't even thought of that," Travis whispered, disappointment in his voice. "Well, that makes me sad. But, if it *has* disappeared, then I need you to tell me how to get another one."

"Oh, dear. That's a problem. At the Invention Convention they only had a few prototypes. They asked everyone who bought one, or in my case, two, to please watch for their future communication and help them spread the word about the

Mind-Boggler when it was in full production. I've never heard from them, and it's been, what? Nine months, a year?"

Travis became even more quiet, but I could hear him thinking. First of all, he was going to ask me for mine. Then, he thought better of that. "Well, then, can I impose upon you *hugely* to come and work your wonders, your mystery-solving wonders, and maybe find it?"

The *Coastal First Nations People* project flew out the bright and sunny window. But I couldn't say no. No. I couldn't say no.

Sighing, as if that would make any difference, I asked, "Which dog park are you at?"

Travis's voice perked right up. "The one nearest you, you know...."

"Yes, I know. I'll be there soon." I disconnected and turned back to the mirror. A rapid bit of damage control was called for. Quick comb through my short hair, and perhaps a dash of mascara and lipstick. Trade my scruffy worn-for-several-days black leggings and black T-shirt, for scruffy *clean* black leggings and black T-shirt.

Robbie jumped down from the window sill and hung close on my heels as I headed for the back door. I knew what that meant. And sure enough....

"Can I come along, Joy, please?" he cajoled.

"But Robbie, it's a dog park. Do you really wanna go where there are a lot of dogs? Some of them may not realize you're a robot and chase you because you look like a cat."

"Travis said the dogs are all gone! And, Joy, it's a bright sunny day!"

"Yes, and … I'll be hanging out with Detective Travis Rusch. As I recall, the two of you do not get along perfectly well."

Robbie swished his tail and shrugged. "I'm totally capable of ignoring him and enjoying the day while the two of you chatter away about the missing Mind-Boggler."

I gave the thought a fleeting moment's attention. Yes, Robbie would enjoy himself out in the sunny day. But I'd have to keep an eye on him, while also addressing Travis's problem. As brilliant as Robbie was, he failed to realize that he was the single most expensive thing I possessed, and I couldn't have him out in a dog park without taking a considerable amount of my attention.

"No, Robbie, I can't be focusing on Travis's problem and have a chunk of my attention fixed on you at the same time. And it's a dog park. More dogs will come. But I'll tell you what, I'll take you to a park sometime very soon, just the two of us."

Robbie gave me a very human look—how does he *do* that?—that said, 'oh yeah, I'm looking forward to that, the first day after never.' But he didn't say anything, he just turned on his little robot kitty heels, swished his tail, and stalked back into the bedroom.

"Bring the car to the back door," I said into my wrist comp. I heard the car start up and move out of the garage as I slipped on my shoes. "Don't be upset Robbie. I won't be long. I'll send you visuals."

"*Great!*" He said from the bedroom, sarcasm dripping from the one word.

I didn't have time to placate a robot at the moment. I stepped out the back door and got in the car. "To the closest dog park."

"Yes, Dr. Forest." The car pulled onto the road. "Are you meeting one of the Ladybirds with their little terriers?"

"That would be fun, wouldn't it? But, no, I'm meeting Travis."

"Oh! Is he working a case?"

"Again, no. Well, not exactly. He's trying to solve a mystery of his own making and has recruited me to help."

"I see," the car said. "Sort of."

"Yeah, that's about where I'm at, too."

\* \*

We soon pulled up to the dog park and as Travis had said, there was not a single dog to be seen. I didn't expect that to be literally true, given this gorgeous day. I spied Travis sitting alone on a bench at the opposite end of the dog park, under a beautiful chestnut tree, leaves bursting forth in profusion, gathering and reflecting the brilliant sunlight.

"He's at the other end of the park. You can drive up to the corner and park."

The car drove to the corner and I climbed out. "Be back in a bit."

"I'll be here," the car quipped.

As I walked toward Travis, I took in the delightful riot of robins. I've never seen so many in one place! The chestnut tree that Travis was under was not the only remarkable tree here. All around the circumference of the dog park were dogwoods, elm trees, and alders, with a few gigantic firs interspersed among them. I took a bit of a detour on my way to Travis to walk by a few of the trees, noting the abundance of homes the robins were industriously crafting. I paused by a lovely little dogwood and communed with the birds for a few moments. Then I turned and headed toward Travis, who still did not seem to be aware of my presence. So unlike him.

At that moment, I watched as he leapt up, got down on his hands and knees, and peered under the bench.

*Weird!* This Mind-Boggler thing really had him rattled.

"*Hey!*" I called.

Travis jumped and smacked his head on the underside of the bench. Standing, while grabbing the back of his head, he looked embarrassed.

Still gorgeous though, darn it. "Are you all right?"

"Hey, Joy. I'm just trying to knock some sense into myself, I guess. Looking for the umpteenth time for that elusive Mind-Boggler. I've looked under this bench half-a-dozen times. But, should I even bother? I have no idea how the thing actually behaves."

"Let's sit," I said sitting and patting the bench beside me. Travis sat. "I'm not sure how it behaves in an unusual situation, either. I always tell mine to go back into its box before I fall asleep. Does it have a mind of its own, and would it go wandering around? I don't think so."

We sat in silence for a few moments, although it was not silent. The robins were engaged in a riot of conversation while building their nests. Soon there'd be more! Little fledgling robins, leaping and falling from their nests, doting parents chirping and calling encouragement as their babies learned to fly.

I breathed deeply the fresh air, loving the warm sun on my face, and *bonus!* Vitamin D and all the other fantastic, healthful, benefits of the sun.

"What do you think, Joy?" Travis asked, an edge of urgency in his voice. "Do you have an intuitive hit about where my Mind-Boggler got to?"

"*Ummm,*" I breathed, soaking up the delicious warmth of the sun. "I just got here, and have not seen the sun in ages. Let me drink it in for a few moments."

"Oh yes, of course. Beautiful day. Drinking sunlight. Carry on."

With my face bathed in the sun, I felt the prayer that I'd been listening to come over me. I recited:

> "*What is life?*
> *Is it the flash of a firefly in the night?*
> *Is it the breath of a buffalo in the winter?*

*Is it the little shadow that runs across the grass*
*And loses itself in the sunset?"* [1]

Travis, still jittery, his fingers tapped on the arm of the bench. "Distracted as I am, that was incredibly beautiful! Did you just make it up on the spur of the moment?"

"No, it's the poem I was listening to, recited by Chief Dan George, when you interrupted my work."

"Ah, I'm a lout. I apologize again, Joy."

I opened my eyes, not wanting to move from the glow of the sunlight, but I must attend to the situation at hand. I turned to sit sideways on the bench, folded up my knees, cross-legged, facing Travis.

There he sat, out of uniform, a rare sight. He wore a western-style green plaid shirt that picked up the green in his alluring, chameleon-color-shifting eyes. Did he even know that? Jeans, and, yes, cowboy boots! Indeed! Cowboy boots!

"You're wearing cowboy boots! I've never seen you wear cowboy boots! And, by the way, they're fantastic."

"Yeah, I call this my incognito outfit. Fake cowboy that I am. I'm a little embarrassed for you to see me dressed like this, given that you were raised on the farm and actually own a horse."

"Ah, well, never mind that! Cowboys don't have a trademark on western clothing. Anyone can wear it, and if they wear it well, *urrr-umm....*" I was close to painting myself into an uncomfortable corner. Unbidden, the thoughts of times he and I had been this close to one another without a hoard of other people around came to mind. I could count the occasions on one hand. I moved away from these contemplations.

"What were you doing when you fell asleep?"

"I was sitting here just exactly like this, more in the center of the bench, and the Mind-Boggler was hovering in front of me, right here, like this," he gestured. "I'm mystified by how I fell into that deep sleep. I was really enjoying interacting with the Mind-Boggler."

"Maybe that's why. For once you were truly relaxed. Your mind off of all those things that are so stressful in your job. You were in the moment and went into more of a trance state than sleep."

Travis nodded. "You must be right, Joy. I was so excited, and then I fell asleep or, as you suggest, fell into a trance." He sighed deeply. Then he added in a quiet voice, "I don't know when I've so utterly enjoyed myself. Not even as a kid. As the oldest child in my family, and with a father whose job took him away from home weeks at a time, I always felt responsible."

Silence fell between us while he contemplated his childhood. Then he continued. "I found myself wondering what it would have been like for me if I'd had a Mind-Boggler when I was a kid. If I understand correctly, it can do more than just expand one's senses. Not that there's anything 'just' about that! It's pretty impressive. While I was communicating with it regarding the colors, I had a feeling that it was waiting for me to become more introspective, and to go deeper. Am I wrong about that?"

"No. You're right." His comment made me contemplate what it might have been like in *my* childhood to have had a Mind-Boggler. A couple of the times my aunt had undone me with her harsh judgments rose to the surface. What if I could have decompressed that pain and confusion with the Mind-Boggler?

Oh, well, not much point in considering that now. The past was over. And my aunt and I had a pretty good relationship these days. She has mellowed, and I live two-hundred miles away. Win-win.

I remained quiet, hoping Travis would share more about his childhood. He'd never mentioned anything about it, and, *was it not fascinating?*

"Were you happy?" I finally asked. "I mean as a child, were you happy?"

Travis shrugged. Oh, I don't know. I suppose I was as happy as any kid who was filled with angst and woe."

I chuckled softly in agreement, thinking to myself, I suspect you were not like *any* kid. As this line of discussion made him melancholy, I shifted the subject. "So, you thought you saw colors beyond your usual range?"

"Oh! Joy, it was so remarkable! I do believe I saw colors that I've never seen. There was one spectacular color, I can see it in my mind, but not in the world around me. How to describe it? It was off of the edge of purple and blue, sort of in that range, so beautiful, and different from anything I've ever seen. That little glimpse makes me want to see it more!"

I nodded. I loved seeing this side of Travis. So different from the somewhat restrained, constrained police detective I usually saw. Not that he didn't have his soft side. Not that we hadn't shared a guffaw or two. Or a dozen. Not that I hadn't, a time or two, felt closer to him than just about anyone in my life.

But not, at the same time, was I ever convinced it would go farther. Never mind all that! Whatever the case may be, we were bonding, in this moment, to a new level of friendship, as he let me see his vulnerable side.

As I smiled at him with these thoughts, feeling closer than ever, I watched as something shifted in his eyes. They dared me to come inside.

A trilling of tiny, shrill barks intruded on our reverie. *What are the odds?* Apparently, very high, as something *always* intruded whenever we approached getting closer. Even on a sunny day, in a dog park, with no one else around.

Well, now there was someone else around.

I looked over at the crew of tiny dogs barking up a storm, with a tiny woman, her back to us, trying to disentangle the leashes of four itty bitty Yorkshire terriers that had leapt from her car.

I couldn't help giggling when I saw it was my little friend, Possum, with, apparently, the pets of the Ladybird Quartet in tow.

She finally turned, with the leashes only marginally disentangled, and the little dogs scurrying forward leaping and barking in glee. Still trying to wrangle them into some semblance of order, she didn't look up until she was practically upon us, sitting on the dog park bench, chuckling. Finally, she looked up. Recognizing us, she was practically beside herself, and the little dogs recognizing me, almost broke their barkers, leaping at their leashes like a school of wild fish, to get to me.

"*Oh! Oh! Oh!*" Possum cried. "Joy! It's you! And … you're with Detective Travis! Together! *So perfect!*"

*Holy jeepers!* This is gonna cause some complication when the Ladybirds get wind of what Possum thinks she's seeing. "Well, no, not exactly 'together.'" Obviously, that didn't make much sense. Here we sat. On a park bench. Together.

"What do you mean, you're not together?" Possum asked over the high-pitched barking of the little dogs, doing her darnedest to disentangle them enough to keep them from strangling each other. "There you sit, on a park bench, side-by-side. Is that not the definition of 'together?'"

I exchanged a look with Travis and rolled my eyes. He grinned that crooked grin of his, only marginally stifling a snicker.

Defeated, I nodded weakly. "I guess that is the commonly accepted definition of 'together.'" Rather than launching into a long and awkward effort at an explanation, I opted to change the subject altogether. "It looks like you have all of the Ladybirds' little terriers."

"I do. Little *terrors* is more like it," Possum laughed. She reached down and unhooked Poofie from her leash, and handed her to me.

"I have Poofie because Sophia has gone to Paris with her daughter. I agreed to take care of Poofie while they were gone with great delight."

"Lavender," Travis said, under his voice.

Poofie squirmed in my grasp and I looked down at her with a serious expression. "Now you sit down and be calm," I told her. She immediately curled up in my lap and looked at the other doggies as though they were behaving very badly.

"Very good!" Possum said to me as she unhooked Wolf from a second leash and handed him to Travis. "See if you can get Wolf to behave as readily as Joy has succeeded in doing with Poofie."

"*Wolf* and *Poofie*? I have received an unfairly fierce dog!" He said, reluctantly taking the little dog and holding him at arms' length, while Wolf squirmed and whined.

"Put him in your lap," I said, "and talk to him softly."

Travis set him on his lap. "Okay, little doggy, you must now behave. See Miss Poofie over there in Joy's lap? Be like that!"

Wolf continued to squirm and whine in Travis's lap.

Possum handed him a packet of doggy treats. "Give him a couple of these and he'll be quite happy."

Travis did as she bid and Wolf calmed down, munching happily.

Gesturing to him, Possum said, "And Mary has some kind of a wedding to attend this weekend. She'll be gone for three days."

"Pink," Travis said.

Poofie, in my lap, began to utter a little growl, looking over at Wolf, happily enjoying his treats. I held my hand out to Travis. "Treats, please."

He gave me a stingy few. "I gotta keep most of them in case he goes off again."

I fed a couple to Poofie. "I'm saving the rest. You can't have them all at once."

Possum sat down on the ground before us, and the two other little Yorkies, Mulder and Scully, climbed into her lap, squabbling over the territory. Possum produced more doggy treats and they settled into bliss. "And Elvira is having some significant dental surgery as we speak, and asked if I'd look after Scully for a couple of days while she recovered."

"Yellow," Travis said.

"Then, when Elgin learned that these three little hooligans would be together, she begged me to let Mulder join them for a happy two-day playdate. Well ... as you can see, I agreed."

"Green," Travis said.

I knew he was reciting the colors that each of the Lady-birds was generally seen wearing, and he was one-hundred percent correct. I was impressed that he had these details in his brain database.

"But what are the odds?!" Possum burst out. "What are the odds? I've never been to this dog park. Why would I? I don't have a dog." Then her brow wrinkled. "But ... Joy, you don't have a dog, either. And, Detective Travis, do you have a dog?" She glanced around the park. "In fact, I don't see a single other dog here."

"Just ... Travis, please. Especially when I'm off duty."

Possum giggled impossibly, clearly overcome by shyness. "Oh, well ... I ... well ... *hmmm.* But you're still a detective."

"Travis, please," he insisted grinning at her.

Candidly, that grin could pretty much knock any woman for a loop, and it just about undid Possum. She buried her face in the woolly fur of Scully. "*O... kay... ahm... T-Travis,*" she stuttered.

One would hardly imagine that this shy, tiny, woman had one of the most beautiful singing voices on earth. But she did.

She gathered her courage and looked up at him from among Scully's fur. I'd never seen her look so cute, her pointy little opossum-like features taking on a glow in a shaft of brilliant sunlight.

My, my, goodness! What was happening here?

Almost as if she heard my thought, and making me feel like an awful, terrible person, she started to stand, exclaiming, "Oh, what is the matter with me? I just come and plop here in the middle of your private tête-à-tête. *I'm so sorry!*"

"No-no-no!" I protested. "We're not having a private tête-à-tête, as such. We're very happy to see you. I haven't seen you in way too long, and you and the little Yorkies are making my day."

"Seconded!" Travis agreed.

"Well if you really don't mind. It's so much of a relief to have a couple of the dogs in other hands, which makes them all manageable. But all of them together ... *whoosh!* They are a handful!"

"They are, indeed," Travis nodded.

"So, Possum, how long will Sophia be in Paris?" I asked.

"She was rather vague. Which certainly surprised me, given how practically unnaturally attached she is to Poofie. Who, I must observe, is remarkably content in your lap," she said with an evil grin.

"Oh no ... you're not going to recruit me to dog sit. I'm on a deadline. It's enough to be distracted by Travis, trying and help him with his stuff." Oh, phooey-padooey, I didn't mean to let that slip.

Possum nodded. "So this is sort of a work meeting?"

"Well, not exactly that either." I didn't want to bring up the Mind-Boggler. I had learned early on not to mention it because everyone always wanted one for themselves. And, well, I did not work for the company. Further, it appeared that the company no longer existed. I glanced at Travis, to see if he was on the same page with me.

He was.

"Anyway," I continued, "we needn't go into that, as it's pretty much Travis's business, and frankly, quite boring."

I heard Travis exclaim in my mind, '*Bor-ing?!*'

I launched on, there was no turning back. "Much more interesting is what the Ladybirds are up to. With Sophia gone, will you be just a quartet?"

"Perhaps. We haven't made any plans, yet. However, as it happens, I'll be soloing at a *huge* church in Seattle in a couple of weeks."

"Oh, Possum, that's fantastic! How did that come about?"

"Some folks were visiting relatives at our church and happened to hear us. For some reason I don't understand, they requested me to sing a couple of solos for a convention they have coming up."

"How wonderful!" I was delighted for her, while at the same time, I wondered how she'd be without her backup, given her timid nature, in addition to having to go away from home. Again, she spoke my thoughts.

"It's very exciting. and ... I'm terrified. Why did I agree? *Why?* It's too late to back out. Short of dropping dead, which I'm sort of wishing would happen, I gotta do it. And that's another reason why it seems fortuitous to bump into you, because, it would really, *really* help me a big whole bunch if you took little Poofie for a couple days. Because if I have to schlep her up there, even though they're putting me up in a very nice hotel, I hate the thought of leaving little Poofie alone in that hotel room for the several hours of rehearsal, and then, all alone during two night's performances. So, if you would, can I impose upon you to take care of Poofie while I'm in Seattle?"

"Of *course*, Possum. I'd be delighted. *And Robbie!* Oh my goodness he'll be thrilled. In fact, if you don't mind, I'd like to tell him right now. He can always check into what I'm doing, but he was so miffed at me for not bringing him to the dog park, regardless of my arguments, that this would really change his mood."

"Yes, please, Joy tell him now," Possum insisted.

I called Robbie from my wrist comp. "Hey there Robbie, do you wanna hear some exciting news?"

"Sure," he said, with a tone of 'but I don't forgive you,' in his voice.

"Possum just happened to show up at the dog park with all the Ladybirds' Yorkshire terriers in tow. I'll give you details later, or you can replay them, but the point is, we'll be taking care of little Poofie, while Possum, who is dog-sitting for Sophia, goes to Seattle to sing in a couple of performances, soloing with her beautiful voice."

"*Oh! Oh! Oh!* So much good news!" Robbie said, his voice changing to transparent joy.

"Yes, lots of fun news. Something to look forward to. I'll tell you more later."

"Can't wait to hear it. I'm not even going to rerun it, I want to hear it from you live."

"It's a deal!" I signed off. Then I had another thought. Wouldn't it be special to go with Possum to Seattle, and see her perform?

The challenging logistics slammed in from every direction. I had just agreed to take care of Poofie. I had also just promised Robbie he was going to get to spend time with Poofie. Thus … I'd be taking Robbie, and Poofie, and Possum, to Seattle. *Hmmm.* Well, it would work out. Robbie could stay with Poofie while I enjoyed Possums' performances.

"What do you think of this idea?" I said, throwing all caution to the winds. "What if Robbie and I joined you? Drove up with you to Seattle? I could attend your performances while Robbie hung out with Poofie."

Possum leaped up, apparently forgetting that she had a lap full of dogs. The little dogs scattered, yelping, as she grabbed me and gave me a huge hug. "Oh, you don't know, Joy, you just don't know! I was distressed about every part of this entire thing, none the least being the whole traveling piece. I was miserable. And now you've made it magical! I was wondering if I was supposed to do it, and now… Out of the blue!… you make it *yes!* I *am* supposed to do it."

"Of *course* you're supposed to do it, dear Possum! That goes without saying. Now you'd better gather those two little dogs that are running off, dragging their leashes."

"Oh, *yikes!* I completely forgot about them!" She turned and chased the little terriers, each having headed in a different direction. While she gathered them together, I looked over at Travis.

"Although it sadly looks as though I'm not gonna get my Mind-Boggler," he said, "I get it that you don't want to talk about it in front of Possum. But I'm curious as to why?…"

"Because whenever I mention it, people always want one for themselves, and, you know, as I told you, the company seems to no longer exist."

"That's what I thought, but I wasn't sure. Here she comes, pups in tow."

It was the cutest sight I ever saw. Like a picture that should be on the cover of a kids' book or a dog magazine, with Possum, grinning, a little Yorkshire terrier under each arm. I swear, the dogs were grinning too. *Cute. Cute. Cute!*

"Okay, y'all, I'm going to leave you now," she said as she came up to us. "You've totally made my day, Joy! I'm going to go home and start poking through my wardrobe, and practicing my songs. I've been avoiding it. Dreading it. Just, dreading it with every fiber of my being, and you've turned it around, one-hundred-and-eighty degrees."

She plucked Poofie and Wolf from Travis and me, hooked them to their leashes, blew us kisses, and headed for her car, which was, coincidentally and strangely, the same as mine, a retrofitted, self-driving, somewhat dated but perfectly serviceable, Forester.

"*Love you!*" She called faintly across the dog park. She herded the dogs into her car and took off.

Travis and I exchanged a look. "Suddenly feels kinda lonely," Travis said.

"Yeah. She leaves a void in the wake of her charming waves."

Travis chuckled as he picked up the little packet of doggy treats that he'd sat down on the bench beside him. "What am I to do with these?"

"Hand them to me. I'll be using them in a couple of weeks when I'm hanging out with Poofie."

"Oh, that's right!" He handed me the doggy treats. "It sounds like a lot of fun, the four of you, Possum, Poofie, Robbie, and you, off to Seattle."

"Yes, it does. And it's been a while since I've had anything resembling a break. But I'll have to hustle to pull things together in order to feel comfortable setting aside my work for two or three days."

"Speaking of which, I suppose you're chomping at the bit to get back to your *Coastal First Nations* research. I guess the Mind-Boggler is just gone."

"Do not despair," I said. He was right—I should get back to work. But I longed to pick up the thread that had been interrupted by Possum, with Travis sharing a little about his childhood. Could we get back to that? I wondered.

The sun began to sink to the west. Long, brilliantly golden molten rays scattered along the grass, casting lengthening shadows of our bench, the spreading chestnut tree, and all the trees surrounding the park. Yes, I would soon go home. But right now, I wanted to spend just a little more time here.

A pair of robins flew into the branches of the tree above us, chattering between themselves. I could just hear the husband saying, "Are you sure about this tree? It has humans sitting under it." And his wife replying, "It'll be fine. It's such a perfect tree and we're high up and safe here among the branches and leaves."

I grinned at my anthropomorphizing the little birds.

"What are you smiling about?" Travis asked.

"I was just imagining the conversation between the two robins that have taken up residence among the branches overhead."

"Oh," Travis replied. "You're so observant! I didn't even notice them."

"You're observant, too! Noting the color that each of the Ladybirds usually wears."

Travis peered into the branches overhead, searching for the pair of robins. "I guess ... we're sort of two little birds of a kind."

"I guess we are, my fine-feathered friend!" I teased. "But, before I go and leave you to your reverie, I was so interested in what you were saying about your childhood before Possum came. Did you always want to be a detective?"

"Not … not exactly. I was probably a pretty strange kid, though apparently, I kept up an acceptable front. What I *truly* wanted to do, and I read every book on the subject …" He interrupted himself and let out a loud guffaw.

I was taken aback. I had no idea what had so tickled his funny bone!

"*What's! So! Funny!?*" I demanded.

"Well, dear Joy, what I wanted to be and do when I was a kid, was to grow up, and essentially, be *YOU!*"

I shook my head. I didn't understand. I usually got things, but he had me here.

"No, he said, reading my mind, "I didn't want to be a woman. I've always liked being a man. What I wanted to do was to solve mysteries. I wanted to have second sight. I wanted to help people. I wanted to solve their problems. I wanted to make them happy, to find their lost things, to find lost people.

"When I was a kid, I'd go to the library in downtown Kansas City where I grew up, and ferret through the old dusty books. I read all the *Hardy Boys* books.…"

"*Oh!*" I exclaimed. This was not usual! These really old books!

"Yes, I found them, and I read them. And not only that, I discovered raggedy, dogeared, beaten, abused, stained Nancy Drew books, too, and read them, every single one."

Well! I could *not* have been more surprised or pleased. We truly were two birds of a kind. "Me too," I said. "I read all of those books, but I also had a fascination with cultures. I wanted to be a missionary. No, that's not right. More accurately, I wanted to be kind of an anti-missionary, you know, to *not* convert people, but instead, to save and protect the beauty of their precious cultures."

"And now you're manifesting all your heart's desires," Travis observed.

He made me pause. "Well, yes. I never thought of it that way but, thanks for pointing it out. You're right. In my humble little cottage, with my little bio cat and my little robot cat, sometimes working around the clock, it *is* the life I dreamed of. You, too, have come very close to your childhood dream. You do all of those things. You make people's lives better, you find lost people, you know, you do all those things."

"Fairly close, but with one exception. And that's where you come in."

"Me?"

"Yes. Of course, you. Who else? The so aptly-named, invincible, and remarkable *Joy* Forest. Always bringing and spreading joy! Always having that insight that solves the mystery. You have the one thing I lack. And that's when I come to you."

I knew what he was going to say.

"And that's … your second sight."

"I knew you were going to say that!"

We laughed.

"But of course," Travis affirmed.

"However," I pointed out, "it's unfortunate that it's a bit erratic, you can't count on it."

"Oh, Joy, I disagree. It *always* comes through. It might take a while, but it always comes through."

I didn't think that was true, but I was willing to let it stand for the moment. "It's *so* lovely you say that, Travis. Even if it's not true, I do love it if I've been helpful to you in your work. I know I've been quite testy many times when you've asked for my help. But, I don't think I realized you were seriously needing my assistance…."

"Oh goodness! How could you not know?" He shook his head in amazement. "Well, now you do."

I nodded. "Now, I know." I chuckled. "Even so, I have to append a disclaimer that this doesn't mean I won't be testy in the future. Because you always do seem to land on me right when…."

"I know, you're on a deadline. But, Joy, seriously, you're *always* on a deadline."

I tried to think of a protestation. But I could not come up with one. I conceded. "You're probably right."

"I am *definitely* right." He feigned a scowl, looking at me from under his eyebrows, daring me to consider further argument.

I felt all glowy. It was lovely to be told in so many words that I was truly needed. My efforts had been accompanied with generous monetary rewards and gifts of gratitude from those who'd been assisted, that Travis handed on to me … money and gifts that I generally gave to those in more need than I. I reminded myself that my conservative lifestyle was of my own making.

A chilly breeze swirled around us, and I shivered. The sun was sinking. Dusk breathed at the edges of the moment. I did not want it to pass. But pass it must.

"Evening approaches," Travis said, an edge of sadness in his voice. "I have the night shift, I should go home and grab a couple hours of sleep before going back out to save lives and the like."

The twittering birds above cooed softly to one another. I pictured them side by side, their fluffy feathers sharing warmth.

Travis stood and stretched, reaching his arms overhead, his trim and toned body complementing his cowboy outfit to the nth degree. *Holy nuns afire*, he was gorgeous!

But off we must hie ourselves, each to our life callings.

"Although I'm most sorry to have lost the precious gift you gave me, the beyond compare Mind-Boggler, this day turned out lovelier than I could have imagined."

The wind picked up a bit as the cool breeze turned into something reminiscent of the recently passed winter.

"May I walk you to your car?" he asked.

"With pleasure. But en route, let us stop off over here at this beautiful dogwood tree, fully inhabited by the charming robins. I need to say goodnight to them, and thank them for something...."

"Thank the robins for something?" Travis asked. "How intriguing."

We amble to the dogwood, filled with cooing twitters of robins settling down to sleep. I reached up among the branches that were just above my head.

"What are you doing?" Travis asked.

In the last sparkling rays of the setting sun, I turned to him and handed him his Mind-Boggler.

"Wha... what? *What?*" He took it, stunned.

"Your Mind-Boggler, carefully attended to this afternoon by one of the residents of this lovely dogwood tree, who believed it would be a great complement to her new home, it had so attracted her attention when it was making all the sounds of herself and her peers, as you instructed it to do. But, without your attention and energy, after a while, it went to sleep. She lost interest in it, but here it sat safe, while you and I shared a lovely afternoon."

"Oh, Joy, you are ... well, words fail me. You knew it was here all along? Why didn't you tell me right away?"

"Because ... because ... I don't know why." But I *did* know. I wanted to spend the afternoon with him. Never mind my endless deadlines, never mind even the Salish Chief's lovely poetry. Never mind any of it. I had known how the day would end. But the great unfolding of all that came in between is the delight and mystery of life.

Travis held his Mind-Boggler close to his chest giving me a look of awe. "Thank you, Joy. *Thank you!*"

"You're always welcome, my friend."

We turned to walk to our vehicles.

Yes, I had to acknowledge I was good at solving mysteries ... except, of course, the one that ruled my heart.

## *The End*

[1]Chief Dan George, "What is Life?"

# A Loveliness
## of
# Ladybugs

*A Joy Forest Cozy Mystery*

# BLYTHE AYNE

In case you've not read *A Loveliness of Ladybugs*, I've included the first chapter here:

# *A Loveliness of Ladybugs*

## *Chapter 1*
## *June 1, 2032*

"**D**etective Travis Rusch," my computer whispered as a small image of Travis appeared in the holo.

Ignoring it, I continued to hammer away at my work like a fiend, *trying* to meet my deadline.

"Detective Travis Rus…."

"I *heard* you," I muttered.

"No need to get snippy," the computer retorted.

"Come on Joy," Travis nagged. "I've got to talk to you."

"*Shi-i-inty.*" I smacked my forehead with my palm. "Hang on, Travis. Give me a moment." I looked at what I'd just written. Now, just—*where was I?* I'd lost my thread. Or Travis lost my thread.

"Connect," I said, resigned to yet another setback to my current project. The image of Travis started to grow. "Small," I ordered. The image shrank. There's distraction, and there's too much distraction. "I'm on deadline, Travis."

"You're always on deadline. Look, I need your help."

Dang, he's gorgeous! A*hm* … don't need *that* thought right now. "You need my help? Let-me-think. *Ah … no.*" I recalled the last time he "needed my help."

"This isn't like that, Joy." He read my mind.

"Of course it isn't. But I can't, Travis. I've got work to do. I'm sure you'll find someone else to … whatever it is."

"It's about Teaspoon."

That stopped me. Of course it would. "Teaspoon? *The* Teaspoon?"

"Yep. The one and only."

That's when I noticed in the tiny holo that Travis stood in my front yard, standing by my lilac bush.

"You're *here.*"

"I am."

"Is it that important, or were you just driving by?"

"It's important. And I was in the neighborhood."

"*Sheesh.*" I disconnected from him. "Mirror." The holo reflected my image. Not a happy picture. I ran my fingers through my hair, pretty much succeeding in making it stand up in slightly different ways than it had been. Sans makeup. Ragged plaid shirt. Ancient sweat pants. Bare feet. Well, you come without an invitation, you get what's here. "Save document and sleep." My words faded to nothing as the holo took a nap.

I went out to the front porch and sat on the top step.

Travis ambled over, taking in my skewed hair and bare feet. "Lookin' great."

"Sarcasm noted. Did you *have* an appointment?"

"Point taken."

"What about Teaspoon?" I demanded, frustrated. *I had work to do.* "This had better be good, Travis. 'Cause if not, this trick will never work again."

"Ariadne is missing."

"*Supplement Village* Ariadne?"

"Is there another?"

"Ahhh, no. Weird. Ariadne is missing. Kind of a relief, yes?" I was a horrible person. A truly horrible person. I didn't mean what I said, of course. But Ariadne Leysi of **Supplement Village** fame would not be missed by me. She created the most obnoxious ads ever imagined, often holding her bitty-little Yorkshire terrier, Teaspoon, hostage, putting the poor dog in the world's goofiest ads, whether she wanted to be or not.

*"Joy!"* Travis shook his head, a small frown passed over his brow.

"I don't mean it."

He sat beside me on the step, pressing a button on his wrist comp. I glanced at the street and watched as the police department's pride, a spanking new Space XXX Roadster, sighed to the ground.

"Whoa! Must be important for you to stop the steed."

"A person is missing. That's always important. Look, I need you to do—whatever it is that you do to get to the bottom of things—your particular brand of …."

"Insight."

"Right. *Insight*. Woo-woo. Second sight. Mystical, magical insight, to see if we can't find her pretty darn fast before the media gets ahold of this. You know how that impinges on my work environment."

"And yet," I noted, "here you are, impinging on *my* work environment, without even a hint of apology." I stretched my toes out into the sunlight, just starting to peek around the clouds. It would be a sunny day.

"Well, sorry. Sort of. But still, a person is missing."

"A high-profile person who, if not found like, right now, will make your life miserable."

"Yeah."

"So, what about Teaspoon?" I asked. "I still don't want to help you look for this woman, who you'll probably discover on a weekend whirl with one of her gorgeous boys."

"There's a reward."

"I don't care about that! Anyway, my getting my current project done will make me more 'reward' than the carrot you're offering."

"Two-hundred thousand dollars, with more pending."

"*Wha-a-at?*" I paused. "*Hmmm* … let me see…." I drew a deep breath. "Yep. Smells like … smells like a publicity stunt. I'll believe that 'reward' when I see it."

Travis punched a few buttons on his wrist comp and up popped a document in the holo between us. He flipped it so it faced me, which said, under the blazing official icon of the Clark County Police:

Deposit: Ariadne Leysi case, Retrieval Reward: $200,000

"Wow," I said softly. "*That* looks real. Who's it from?"

"It's real." He shut off the holo. "It's anonymous. But I tracked it to **Supplement Village**. The one on this side of town. I think it must have come from the family."

"Yeah. Okay. Still seems like a setup. A setup for one of her goofy ads, and you're going to be caught in the middle of it, and you're going to look *goofy*!"

"Except—one word. Teaspoon."

"What about Teaspoon?"

"The note about Ariadne's disappearance mentioned more concern for Teaspoon than Ariadne. Anyway, the creature is alone in the house. No one to feed it…."

"No one to feed *her*." I was a stickler for respecting animals and not calling them "it."

Travis grinned his half-crooked grin. "Right. *Her*. Anyway, the animal has been unfed since, well, whenever. And I can't be chasing after a dog. I'm trying to find a person. I thought you…."

"You thought I'd break and enter and rescue the little dog."

"I'm not saying that."

"Of course not." I considered the gated community where everyone knew Ariadne lived. "Craptastic, Travis, I'll have to get through that gate at her ta-ta Mac-mansion community."

His wrist comp started rattling off some code, and he stood, rattling code back as he engaged the roadster. "You'll figure it out." He hurried down the path, and the Space XXX Roadster lifted into the air.

"*Grrr*," I growled. He knew me too well. I could pass on thinking about Ariadne. Not because I'm completely insensitive, but because I knew Travis would find her. Probably. However, I could *not* do anything now but check on Teaspoon, defenseless, starving little creature.

A little dog needed me!

## *About the Author:*

Thank you for reading the novella of *A Round of Robins*. Be sure to read all of Joy Forest's mysterious near-future adventures, and watch for the novel-length version of *A Round of Robins, coming soon!*

Here's a bit about me, if you're curious. I live near where Joy lives, but I'm in the present, about ten years before where Joy's story begins. Unless you're reading this ten years from now, and then, well, I'm in the past, and you're in Joy's present.

I live in the midst (and often the mist) of ten acres of forest, with domestic and wild creatures as family and companions. Here I create an ever-growing inventory of fiction and nonfiction books, short stories, illustrated kid's books, vast amounts of poetry, and the occasional article. I've also begun audio recording my books, which, having a background in performance, I find quite enjoyable.

I throw a bit of wood carving in when I need a change of pace. And I'm frequently on a ladder, cleaning my gutters. There's something spectacular about being on a ladder—the vista opens up all around, and one feels rather like a bird or a squirrel, perched on a metal branch.

After I received my Doctorate from the University of California at Irvine in the School of Social Sciences, (majoring in psychology and ethnography—surprisingly similar to Joy's scholarly background), I moved to the Pacific Northwest to write and to have a modest private psychotherapy practice in a small town not much bigger than a village.

Finally, I decided it was time to put my full focus on my writing, where, through the world-shrinking internet, I could "meet" greater numbers of people. *Where I could meet you!*

All the creatures in my forest and I are glad you "stopped by." Thank you so much for any reviews or comments you may share. We writers create in a void, and hearing from *YOU* makes all the difference.

*Blythe@BlytheAyne.com*

And here's my website:

*www.BlytheAyne.com*

and my *Boutique of Books*:

https://shop.BlytheAyne.com

*'Til We Meet Again,*
*Blythe*

## Books & Audiobooks by Blythe Ayne

### Fiction:
#### Joy Forest Cozy Mystery Series
A Loveliness of Ladybugs
A Haras of Horses
A Clowder of Cats
A Gaggle of Geese
A Round of Robins - The Novella
A Round of Robins

#### The Darling Undesirables Series:
The Heart of Leo - short story prequel
The Darling Undesirables
Moons Rising
The Inventor's Clone
Heart's Quest

### Novel:
Eos, The Long Dark Road of Horse and Human

### YA Series – The City Under Seattle
#### With Thea Thomas:
The People in the Mirror
Millie in the Mirror
The Angel in the Mirror

#### Middle Grade Novel:
Matthew's Forest

#### Novellas & Short Story Collections:
5 Minute Stories
13 Lovely Frights for Lonely Nights
When Fields Hum And Glow

#### Children's Illustrated Books:
The Rat Who Didn't Like Rats
The Rat Who Didn't Like Christmas

### Nonfiction:
#### How to Save Your Life Series:
Save Your Life with Basic Baking Soda
Save Your Life with Awesome Apple Cider Vinegar
Save Your Life with the Dynamic Duo – D3 and K2
Save Your Life With The Power Of pH Balance
Save Your Life With The Phenomenal Lemon
Save Your Life with Stupendous Spices
Save Your Life with the Elixir of Water